This book belongs to:

Nimait ZQ4

To Lucas, Eli, and all train-o-philes,
big and small.
-*O. C.*

To my lovely wife, Tiffany.
-*H. M.*

Text Copyright ©2007 Oliver Chin
Illustrations Copyright ©2007 Heath McPherson

immedium

Immedium, Inc., P.O. Box 31846, San Francisco, CA 94131
www.immedium.com

First hardcover edition published 2007.

Edited by Tracy Swedlow
Book design by Elaine Chu

Printed in Singapore
10 9 8 7 6 5 4 3 2 1

Library of Congress Cataloging-in-Publication Data

Chin, Oliver Clyde, 1969-
    Timmy and Tammy's train of thought / by Oliver Chin ; illustrated by
Heath McPherson.
       p. cm.
    Summary: Timmy and Tammy love to play with toy trains and hear
train stories, and when their parents take them on a real train ride the
experience is everything they imagined it could be.
    ISBN-13: 978-1-59702-008-4 (hardcover)
    [1. Railroads--Trains--Fiction. 2. Brothers and sisters--Fiction.]
I. McPherson, Heath, ill. II. Title.
PZ7.C44235Tim 2007
[Fic]--dc22

2006024133

ISBN 13: 978-1-59702-008-4

TIMMY AND TAMMY'S TRAIN OF THOUGHT

immedium
Immedium, Inc. · San Francisco

By **Oliver Chin**
Illustrated by **Heath McPherson**

Timmy and his sister Tammy loved trains. Playing on the living room floor, the two pushed their trains along the tracks.

"Choo, Choo!" they whistled.

Timmy adored Wayne the Train.
Tammy fancied Jane.

They both liked Kate and Nate
the freight cars, Hank and Frank
the tank cars, Bruce the Caboose,
and others too.

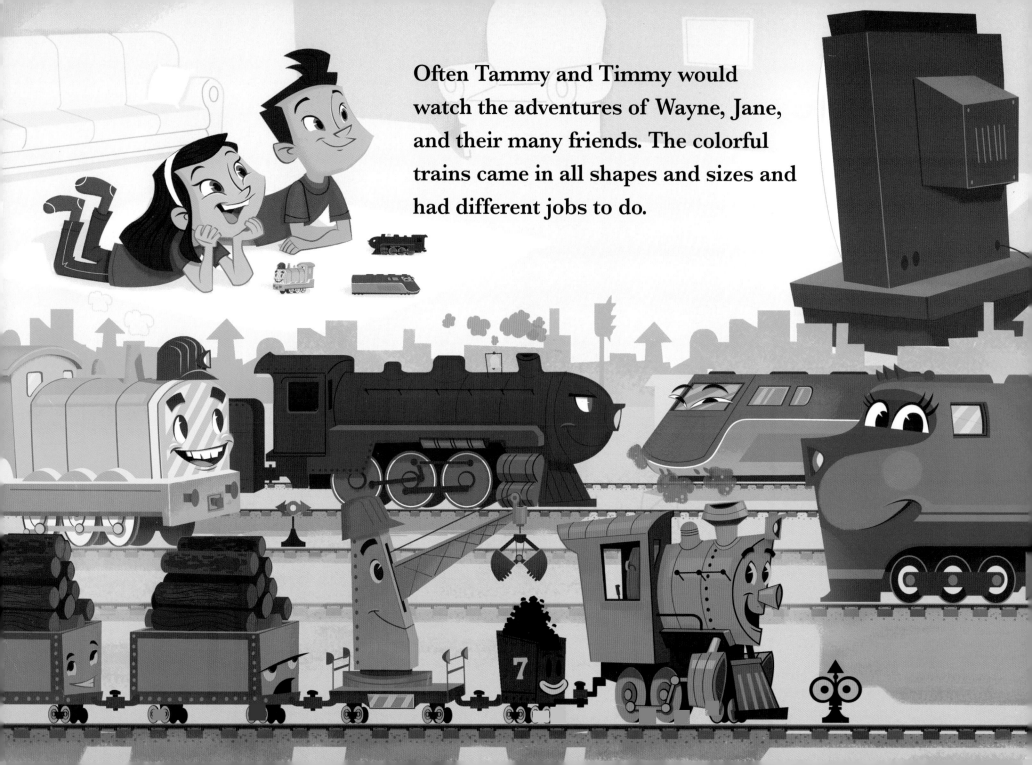

Often Tammy and Timmy would watch the adventures of Wayne, Jane, and their many friends. The colorful trains came in all shapes and sizes and had different jobs to do.

At night, Mom and Dad would read them their favorite bedtime stories. Timmy and Tammy liked hearing the funny sounds the trains made.

Woo! Woo!

Then one day, Mom said, "I think Timmy and Tammy would enjoy riding on a real train."

Dad replied, "That's a great idea. Let's plan a trip!" So they told their children, who became very excited.

On the night before their special
train ride, Timmy dreamt:
"I want to be the engineer!"

Meanwhile, Tammy imagined:
"I want to be the conductor!"

The following day, the family arrived early at the train station. Mom and Dad bought the tickets, and Tammy and Timmy eagerly waited in line.

Barreling through a
billow of smoke,
here came the train!

Timmy and Tammy carefully
chose their seats, and Mom and
Dad sat down behind them.

The conductor punched their tickets and made sure everyone was safely seated.

Next the engineer shouted, "All-Aboard!"
Then they were off!

Timmy and Tammy felt bigger than ever as the little train pulled out beyond the orange cones.

"Toot, Toot!" piped the train.

From the freight yard, the train
moved faster and faster. Passing the
repair shop, roundhouse, and water tank,
it entered a beautiful green forest.

Feeling the cool breeze in their hair, Timmy and Tammy gazed up at the leafy trees around them.

"Shhh, Shhh!" whooshed the train.

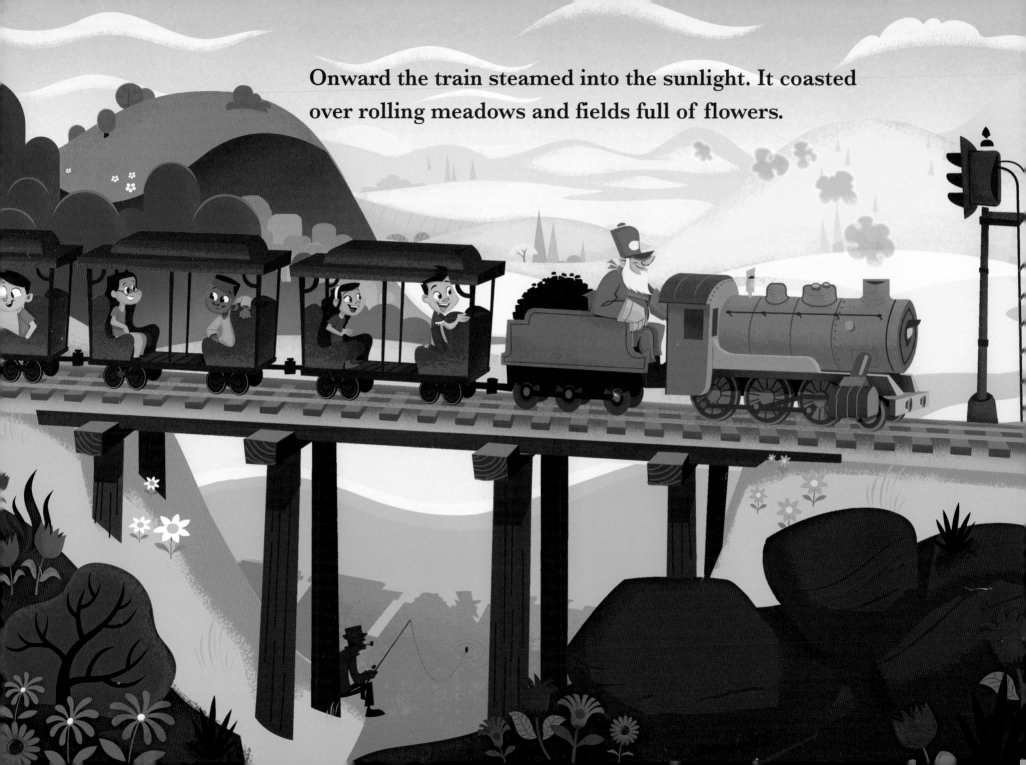

Onward the train steamed into the sunlight. It coasted over rolling meadows and fields full of flowers.

Timmy counted the birds circling overhead. Tammy marveled at the white cotton clouds in the sky.

"Puff, Puff!" huffed the train.

The train rolled through
the park, where people rode
horses, picnicked on benches,
and played games on the grass.

As Tammy watched the spinning carousel, Timmy noticed the engine's golden bell begin to swing.

"Ring, Ring!" chimed the train.

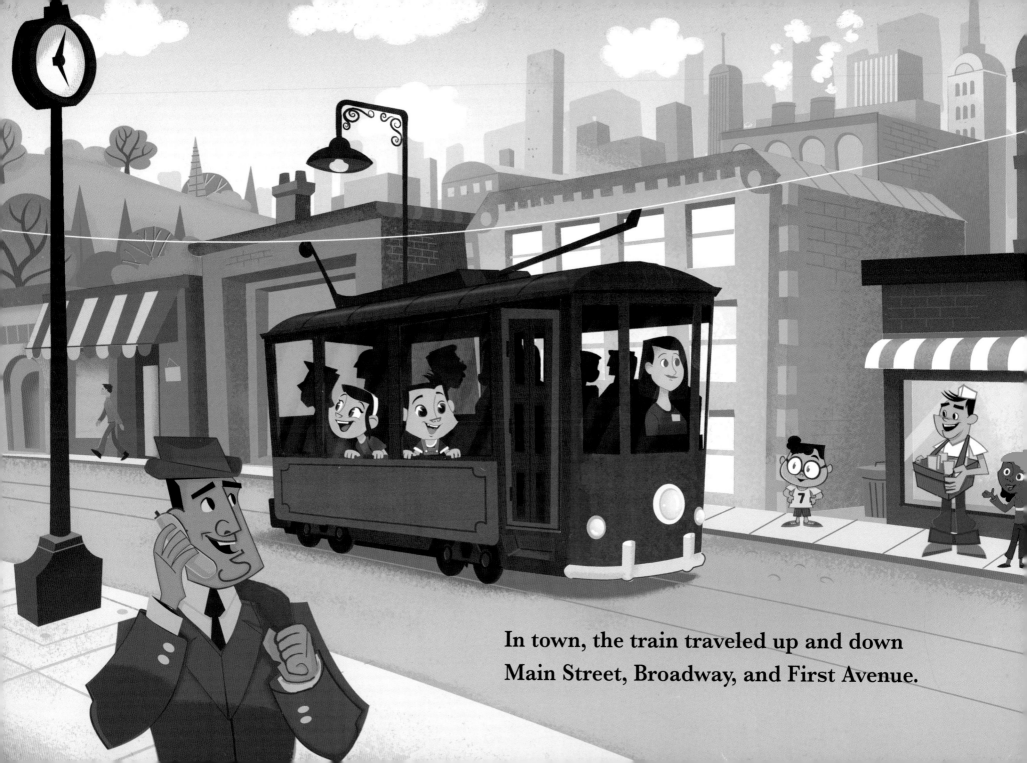

In town, the train traveled up and down
Main Street, Broadway, and First Avenue.

Timmy spotted the post office and its blue mailboxes. Tammy pointed out the courthouse and general store.

"Buzz, Buzz!" hummed the train.

The train climbed the hills to see the city's sights. It reached famous fountains, bronze statues, and tall towers.

Tammy and Timmy waved at the crowds of curious tourists who strolled on the sidewalk.

"Ding-a-ling, Ding-a-ling!" sang the train.

Soon the train approached a dark
tunnel. The engine disappeared
inside, and the rest of the cars trailed
close behind.

As noises echoed loudly in the blackness,
Timmy and Tammy saw the light get
bigger at the other end.

"Whoo, Whoo!" called the train.

Afterwards, the train neared a railroad crossing. Suddenly the arms of the crossing guard came down, an alarm rang urgently, and red lights flashed!

The traffic quickly stopped on both sides of the tracks. Tammy and Timmy both held their breath.

220

RAILROAD CROSSING

"Honk, Honk!" blew the train.

Before long, the train crossed over a long brown bridge, which spanned a rushing river.

Timmy stared at the water far
below. Tammy felt as if she were
flying like a bird.

"Bling, Bling!" beeped the train.

The train rode along a gray highway. It raced beside the speeding cars and trucks.

Timmy and Tammy looked at the blur of lights and wheels across the winding road.

"Chugga, Chugga!" roared the train.

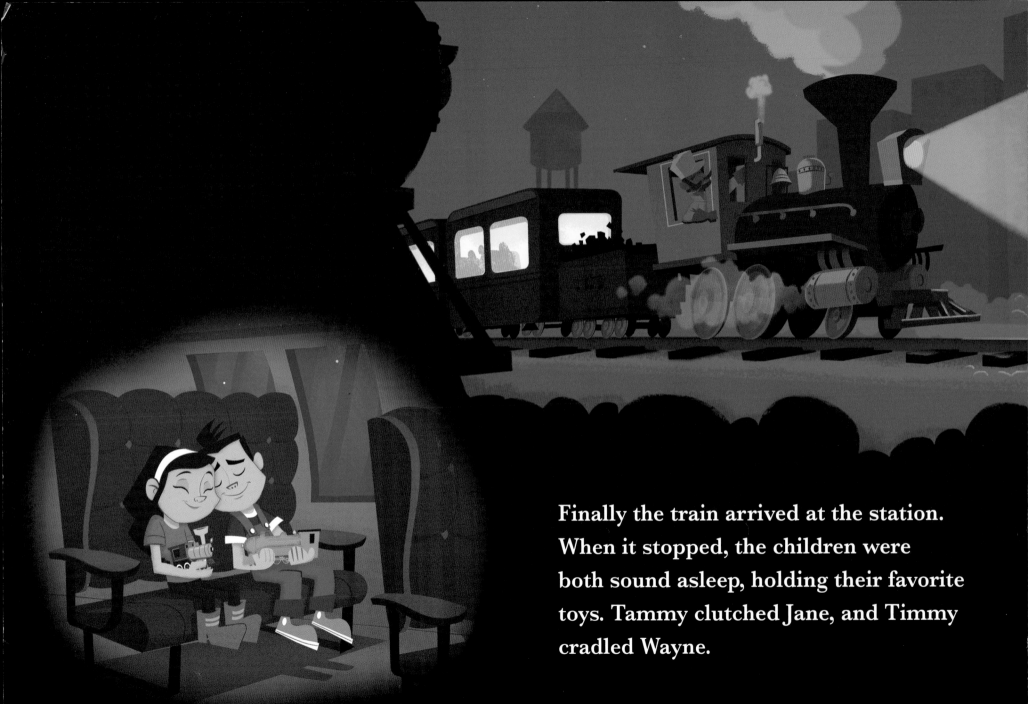

Finally the train arrived at the station. When it stopped, the children were both sound asleep, holding their favorite toys. Tammy clutched Jane, and Timmy cradled Wayne.

TRAIN MUSEUM

Quietly Mom and Dad carried their little
conductor and engineer off the train.

"Hush, Hush!" whispered the train.

Goodbye and see you next time!